For Helen, and a big
thank you to Adélie
for her help
A.S.

♥IREAD
皮皮與波西：晚安小青蛙

繪　　　圖	阿克賽爾‧薛弗勒
譯　　　者	酪梨壽司

發 行 人	劉振強
出 版 者	三民書局股份有限公司
地　　　址	臺北市復興北路 386 號 (復北門市)
	臺北市重慶南路一段 61 號 (重南門市)
電　　　話	(02)25006600
網　　　址	三民網路書店 https://www.sanmin.com.tw

出版日期	初版一刷 2016 年 1 月
	初版五刷 2022 年 4 月
書籍編號	S858161
I S B N	978-957-14-6109-0

Originally published in the English language as PIP AND POSY:
THE BEDTIME FROG
Text Copyright © Nosy Crow 2013
Illustration Copyright © Axel Scheffler 2013
Copyright licensed by Nosy Crow Ltd.
Chinese translation right © 2016 San Min Book Co., Ltd.

小山丘官網

皮皮與波西
晚安小青蛙

阿克賽爾·薛弗勒／圖　　酪梨壽司／譯

小山丘　　

波ㄅㄛ西ㄒㄧ要ㄧㄠ去ㄑㄩ皮ㄆㄧ皮ㄆㄧ家ㄐㄧㄚ住ㄓㄨ一ㄧ晚ㄨㄢ。

她打包得很仔細，不想忘了
任何東西。

她搭上公車，興奮極了。

見到波西，皮皮非常高興。
他大叫：「嗨，波西！」

波西也咯咯笑著說：「哈囉，皮皮！」

皮皮和波西玩得好開心。
他們玩皮皮的小汽車。

他們打造了一個迷你農場。

然後他們玩「海盜看醫生」的遊戲。

他們吃了義大利麵。

他們洗了泡泡澡。

他們刷了牙。

他們讀了
一個好笑的故事。
接著，該上床
睡覺了。

皮皮抱著心愛的小豬玩偶
說：「晚安，波西。」

波（ㄅㄛ）西（ㄒㄧ）說（ㄕㄨㄛ）：「晚（ㄨㄢ）安（ㄢ），皮（ㄆㄧ）皮（ㄆㄧ）。」

他（ㄊㄚ）們（ㄇㄣ）關（ㄍㄨㄢ）了（ㄌㄜ）燈（ㄉㄥ）。

皮皮快睡著時，聽到有個聲音大喊：「小青蛙！」

原來是波西。

「我忘了帶小青蛙，」她小聲啜泣。

「沒有小青蛙我睡不著！」

皮皮把燈打開。他問：
「妳想要這隻泰迪熊嗎，波西？」

但波西不想要皮皮的泰迪熊。
「它不是綠色的。」波西說。
「我的青蛙是綠色的。」

「妳想要我的恐龍嗎?」皮皮又問。
「它是綠色的。」

「不要!」波西回答。
「你的恐龍
太大又太嚇人了!」

「我的青蛙存錢筒呢？」皮皮再問。

「不要！」波西回答，
「那不是我要的青蛙！」

波西哭了，一直哭一直哭。

喔，天啊！可憐的波西！

皮皮想了想，
然後做出一個艱難的決定。

「妳想要小豬嗎，波西?」他問。

波西不哭了。
小豬是一隻超棒的豬。

「好啊，皮皮，請給我小豬。」她回答。

皮皮很快就睡著了。

波西也是。

第二天，
波西回家以後，
她發現她的青蛙……

……還好端端待在原來的地方。

太棒啦！

Posy was going to
stay at Pip's house.

She packed up her suitcase very carefully.
She didn't want to forget anything.

Then she got on the bus.
She was very excited.

Hoppy Holidays!

Pip was really happy
to see Posy.
"Hi, Posy!" he called.

"Hello, Pip!" giggled Posy.

Pip and Posy had lots of fun.
They played with Pip's cars.

They played with the farm.

And then they played a game called
'pirates in hospital'.

They ate spaghetti.

They brushed their teeth.

They had a bubbly bath.

And they read a funny story. After that, it was time for bed.

"Night-night, Posy," said Pip, as he cuddled up with his piggy.

"Sweet dreams, Pip," said Posy.

They switched off their lights.

Pip was very nearly asleep
when he heard a voice.
"Froggy!" said the voice.

It was Posy.
"I've forgotten Froggy," she sniffed.

"I CAN'T SLEEP WITHOUT MY FROGGY!!"

Pip turned his light back on again.
"Would you like this teddy, Posy?" he said.

But Posy did not want Pip's teddy.
"It's not green," she said.
"My frog is green."

"Would you like my dinosaur?" said Pip.
"He's green."

"No!" said Posy.
"That dinosaur
is too big and too scary!"

"What about my frog money box?" said Pip.

"No!" said Posy,
"That is the WRONG FROG!"

Posy cried and cried and cried.

Oh dear! Poor Posy.

Pip thought for a moment.
Then he did a **very difficult** thing.

Posy stopped crying.
Piggy was an extremely nice pig.

"Would you like Piggy, Posy?" he said.

"Yes, please, Pip," she said.

Soon Pip was asleep.

And so was Posy.

And the next day, when Posy went home to her house, she found her frog . . .

. . . exactly where she had left him!

Hooray!

阿克賽爾・薛弗勒　Axel Scheffler

1957年出生於德國漢堡市，25歲時前往英國就讀巴斯藝術學院。他的插畫風格幽默又不失優雅，最著名的當屬《古飛樂》(Gruffalo) 系列作品，不僅榮獲英國多項繪本大獎，譯作超過40種語言，還曾改編為動畫，深受全球觀眾喜愛，是世界知名的繪本作家。薛弗勒現居英國，持續創作中。

酪梨壽司

當過記者、玩過行銷，在紐約和東京流浪多年後，終於返鄉定居的臺灣媽媽。出沒於臉書專頁「酪梨壽司」與個人部落格「酪梨壽司的日記」。